Contents

1

The Tug-of-war

Compere Lion was wandering in the forest one day when he met the elephant. He was taken aback. He had seen all the other animals except the elephant and he was astonished at the size of this creature over whom he was supposed to be king. He eyed the elephant stealthily and he said to himself, 'I wonder who he is?' Anyway, he put on a pleasant face and said, 'Good morning.'

'Good morning, Compere Lion.'

Compere Lion was even more surprised. The elephant did not only know him but knew his name.

He cleared his throat. 'Ah. Hm. You are from round here?'

'No, Compere. I'm from Asia, really. Just thought I'd come over to Africa for a few weeks.'

'Oh, I see,' said Compere Lion. Then, as if he wasn't really asking a question, he said, 'Who is the King of Beasts over there?'

'Well, me,' was the reply.

The lion was astonished, firstly because he had thought that of all the beasts he was the only king. Apart from that, he could not understand it, because there was nothing like the look of royalty about the elephant. And as for the dignity and bearing of a king! The lion all but laughed. Where was this place called Asia? Where was this country in which they could have such a clumsy-looking beast as the elephant as a king?

He pondered and said to himself, 'There is only one thing that could have gained him that title. He is very big and maybe he has great strength. If I show all the animals in Asia as well as my own subjects here that I am the stronger, then I shall be acclaimed king over all the animals in the world.'

Compere Lion glanced at the great size of the elephant. He knew that in his kingdom he was the strongest beast, but as for matching strength with this monster — well, that was a different story.

A strange squint came over his face. He was thinking hard. He was going to arrange a trial of strength and, what was more, he was going to win. He thought of all sorts of dishonest schemes, and at last an idea came to him.

He said, looking casual, 'My friend, you look as if you are good at tug-of-war.'

The elephant grunted, 'It is a game I like but I can't find anyone to pull against me, so I am out of practice.'

'It is all right,' said Compere Lion, 'I will pull against you. I will pull against anybody in friendship. With me, it does not matter who pulls who over the line. I mention this because it is near time for our annual games, and I thought that, since I am the King of Beasts in Africa and you are the King of Beasts over in Asia, we could have a little tug-of-war together at the games. Just for the merriment of our subjects. We will invite all the animals in your kingdom to join with mine in my kingdom, and what better way to salute our subjects than with a game of tug-of-war?'

'That will be very nice,' grunted the elephant, and he chuckled a chuckle that was like the gurgling of a river. 'That will be very good. I will bring all my subjects to your annual games and all the animals in the world will be happy to see us pulling against each other in friendship.'

'Indeed,' said the lion. 'Indeed.' He liked the way the elephant had said 'pulling against each other in friendship.' His brain was working fast.

Shortly afterwards, when the elephant was out walking by himself, the lion called all his subjects together and told them that he was organising games for all the animals in the world. He said the elephant was bringing all his subjects from Asia and the highlight of the games would be a tug-of-war match between himself and the elephant, who was King of Beasts in Asia.

When he made this announcement the monkey fell off a branch.

No one heard the fall because there was such thunderous cheering from the other animals. The monkey brushed his behind and said now, 'Compere, the elephant is so big he will pull you like nothing.'

Everyone looked round, stunned by the monkey's rashness. For Compere Lion never liked any criticism of himself. They all waited to see what Compere Lion would do.

But Compere Lion answered very calmly. He said, 'It is all right. I am the King of Beasts here and he is the King of Beasts in Asia. If he pulls me, I will give him my crown and he will be the King of Beasts of all the World.'

'No, Compere Lion!' the animals shouted as if in chorus. '*You* are the King of Beasts of all the World.'

It was not that they were so fond of Compere Lion. In fact, they were secretly glad at the prospect of the elephant beating him. But they were so scared of him that they had to pretend they could not do without him.

The monkey was silent. He knew all the tricks in the world but he could not guess which one Compere Lion was up to now. But the compere was up to some trick. That was certain. For Compere Lion would never pit himself against the elephant in a fair tug-of-war. Especially where the title 'King of Beasts' was at stake. And especially in front of all the animals in the world. As he scratched his head, trying to work it out, Compere Lion interrupted his thoughts.

'Anyway, Mr Elephant is our guest, and you all must not make him feel badly because, as you see, he came all the way from Asia. Besides, he is a king too. Never mind . . .' He checked himself. Then he went on, 'Mr Elephant is my good friend and I have already told him about the competition. There will be games for everybody — all sorts of games. So what you have to do is to practise. Remember that all the animals from Asia will be coming. We must have the grandest games in honour of our guests.'

The games of the animals opened very grandly indeed. Every one of the animals was taking part, and those from Asia were mingled with all the other animals in the world. The venue was a large clearing in the forest and there were events without a break. To start with, there was a flat race between the horse and the jack-ass, which the horse won because the jack-ass went off in the opposite direction. The cheetah and the gazelle dominated the special sprints, and the Bengal tiger edged out the puma in one of the longer distances. The panther created a sensation by beating the antelope in the closest finish imaginable. He won by a whisker!

Meanwhile, there were swimming races in the nearby river, and the latest news from that end was that Compere Alligator was winning all the medals. The trophy for eating balatas went to

Compere Monkey, who, although the contest was over, was still eating balatas.

Between gobbling down balatas, Compere Monkey was helping the scorer to cheat, so much so that instead of the animals from Asia being far away in the lead, when they counted up the points with the last event remaining, the animals from Asia had scored exactly the same number of points as the other animals in the world.

And so every creature now held his breath, for this was the great moment of the games — the moment for the tug-of-war between Compere Elephant and Compere Lion.

The great plaited rope-vine was placed in the centre of the arena and now the elephant made an appearance at the far end. Although Compere Lion had told the elephant that it did not matter who pulled who over the line, the cheering of the animals from Asia had so excited the elephant that he was now making all sorts of antics such as jumping around, lifting his great hooves in the air, in salute, and limbering up by going up and down on his haunches.

Meanwhile, Compere Lion could not be seen and the animals from Asia were beginning to think that he was afraid. But word got round that he was in a secret part of the forest, practising.

The conch blew his shell and everybody called, 'Compere Lion!' The forest echoed back, 'Compere Lion!' Everyone was getting anxious, but just as they were sending scouts into the forest to look for him, Compere Lion sprang out into the clearing. There was deafening applause from most of the animals in the world.

The huge rope strung out in the middle of the arena touched the forest at Compere Lion's end. Compere Lion had made sure of that. When he was said to be practising in a secret part of the forest, it was no fib. He really had been practising, in a sort of way.

That secret part of the forest was just beyond his side of the clearing, and he had been practising to tie one end of the rope around the trunk of a hog-plum tree!

Not a soul knew of this, apart from Compere Lion and God — and the monkey! Yes, Compere Monkey. Compere Monkey, who knew all the tricks in the world (and had tried most of them himself) had not rested since the day of Compere Lion's announcement. And today he had looked all over the forest, jumping from tree to tree, scratching his head and peering down between the leaves to see if he could catch Compere Lion in any monkey business. When he had reached the hog-plum tree he had hardly crammed half-a-dozen hog-plums into his mouth before he spotted Compere Lion below.

Compere Monkey had coiled his tail around the branch and swung, the better to see. Then he clapped his front paws, because he liked a good trick.

Now he sat back among the leaves, crammed his mouth with hog-plums, and looked down on Compere Lion. All this he did very, very quietly. He even swallowed the hog-plum seeds so that he should not drop them.

After Compere Lion had tied the end of the rope round the hog-plum tree, he had taken the other end to the edge of the forest, lain down on his belly, and tied that end to the tug-of-war rope. And it was at this time that he had skipped out into the clearing.

Compere Monkey, who had observed all this, almost died with laughter. From his perch atop the hog-plum tree he also had a good view of the arena and now he could see Compere Elephant and Compere Lion getting ready to start their contest. As he looked down upon all the animals in the world, they were like a sea of heads and tails and horns, and he could hear the tumult of

7

the shrieks and whistles and grunts and bellows which seemed to drown out all the other noises in the world.

But now there was a sudden hush as the contest was about to start. Everything remained still. Even the jaws of Compere Monkey remained motionless, although hog-plum seeds fell from his open mouth. Of course *he* knew what was going to happen!

A shrill voice broke the silence, 'Everybody ready?' Eyes looked towards Compere Elephant, then at Compere Lion. 'Everybody ready? You know the rules of the game. Take the strain. Ready, steady, go-o!'

This was the voice of Compere Zebra, the referee in the striped suit. He now backed away gracefully, bowing, but no one was

taking any notice of him, for the tug-of-war contest had begun.

Immediately, the elephant took a deep breath and heaved, and he expected to just walk away, dragging the lion over the line. But not so. They both remained exactly as they were, the lion on the edge of the forest, his face strained, grimacing as much as he could, while the elephant was caught like a statue in the posture of walking away.

Shock and astonishment were on the faces of all the animals in the world. In comparison with the massive elephant, Compere Lion looked a tiny, insubstantial beast, and yet the elephant could make no headway against him.

Everyone gazed in breathless wonder. All the noise, all the merriment of the animals from Asia vanished. When these animals had heard the referee say, 'Ready, steady, go-o!' they had been on the point of running out into the arena to crown the elephant 'King of Beasts,' but now only pain and humiliation marked their faces.

Meanwhile, all the other animals in the world were suddenly proud and devoted to Compere Lion, bellowing out his name so loudly that the monkey had to put his paws to his ears.

They shouted out encouragement to Compere Lion, urging him to put in a little extra force to move Compere Elephant, but even after a few minutes the position was the same. The rope remained motionless — the contest dead even.

The elephant worked himself up into desperation. He strained and pulled with every muscle, the agony reddening his eyes, the veins bulging out against the great pillars of his legs.

The lion, on the other hand, leaned back on the rope and bared his teeth and growled and made all sorts of antics with his head. All the onlookers believed he was pulling his guts out. None, except Compere Lion himself, and God — and the monkey — knew what was really happening.

The monkey spat out hog-plum seeds and threw his head back and laughed. He laughed and laughed until he felt his body shake, and the leaves of the trees shake. He kept his eyes fixed on Compere Lion, and he shook his head. What a great actor this imposter was! The beast now had his eyes closed, and his mane was hanging dishevelled over his face and over the front paws which were gripping the ropes. His hind paws were dug into the ground in front of him.

'Pull, Compere Lion, pull!' The chorus of animals sounded like thunder.

Compere Monkey glanced down at the elephant, who was now jumping and kicking to jerk his weight back — not that he was getting any results. He stopped, then stamped on the ground, and the monkey was both amazed and amused to see how the elephant began prancing and grunting and puffing in desperation — puffing so powerfully that Compere Monkey felt sure that it was this which was causing all the leaves around to rustle so violently, and his own tail to tremble. The elephant's great hooves were making big holes in the arena.

This was bringing the uproar to fever pitch, but Compere Monkey was now so weak with laughing that he rested back on the branch. Also, he was feeling a bit jealous, because he felt himself outshone by the trickery of Compere Lion. He lay back very quietly. But, although he was quiet, the leaves and branches were shaking so much more than before that Compere Monkey looked around him, then looked down. The elephant was tugging and prancing, but Compere Monkey had already seen him at this. Also, there was not much wind now, and he noticed that the other trees were quiet. But his tree was shaking more and more, and even rocking.

'What happening, boy?' he said to himself. He looked down and, sure enough, the whole hog-plum tree was shaking and rocking, and presently there was a loud creak.

'What happening, boy?' he said again, alarmed.

Quickly he turned around and looked for another tree to jump onto, but the hog-plum tree creaked more loudly this time, and Compere Monkey was panic-stricken. He held on tightly to a branch and the next moment the tree did not creak but groaned, and Compere Monkey felt himself rocked as though in a cradle. The elephant pulled and pranced now as though mad, and the hog-plum tree made such a great noise that this noise was drowned only by the noises of all the animals from Asia. Compere Elephant was so encouraged by the ground he had gained that he grunted loudly and pranced and tugged even harder, and the groan of the tree and the cheering of the animals from Asia made so great a noise that the forest had never heard the like of it before. Pandemonium reigned as the lion was being pulled inch by inch towards the line. Bewildered, the monkey could not notice this, for he now found himself riding through the air.

For the elephant had made a final heave and a tug, and now the monkey heard a clattering, shattering noise below him. The conch blew his shell and cried, 'Look out!' and the forest echoed, 'Look out!' and Compere Monkey, desperate, hooked his tail onto the branch of a tree he was passing and he remained suspended in the air.

But the hog-plum tree went on its way, and it was only now, when it came crashing down before all the animals in the world, yes, it was only now that all the animals in the world realised what a trick Compere Lion had played.

2

One pitch-black night

I was visiting Mayaro because it was concert night at the Roman Catholic School. The school was under the palms at St Ann's by the sea, and folk coming from all directions usually went there to see the school concert.

I was staying with my old aunt at Plaisance, and Plaisance was only two miles from the school, going due south by way of the beach road. The beach road was a lovely, picturesque road in the day-time, but a little dismal at night. I did not mind it, though. I much preferred it, for the distance was much shorter than going up to the village junction at Quarters, then taking the Guayaguayare road up to School Road, then turning in to walk another half-mile to the school on a desolate road that had no houses. But my old aunt kept on saying all the time she did not like the beach road, and what a frightening road at night the beach road was.

At one stage I said, 'But what's so frightening about the beach road, Tantie?'

She replied, 'Look, I ain't tell you before, but I telling you now. That beach road is a spooky road. You know what is soucouyant? Well that beach road have plenty soucouyant. It have three old ladies living by the bridge, across the river, and all three ah them is soucouyant!'

'But Tantie, how could you believe in soucouyant — how could old ladies fly at night, and go into people's houses, and to the bed where they sleeping? What for?'

'To suck their blood?'

I laughed heartily.

My old aunt said, 'Oh, you don't believe? Well, go on! Anyway, you won't catch me going down there.'

'So you ain't going with me to the concert, Tantie?'

'Me? I'm not going down that beach road.'

I looked at her, and then I said reluctantly, 'Okay then, we'll pass round through Quarters.'

She simply gazed through the window. I was surprised, for I thought she was going to be pleased. I said, 'But Tantie, I'll pass on the other road. The road you want. You said. . .'

She looked at me, 'That distance so far! Me body too old for that. I can't make that. Look, if the concert was in the day I'd go with you, passing on the beach. But not tonight. Not after dark.'

I shook my head. These old-timers were so steeped in all kinds of superstition that it would be folly to try to make them see the light. The concert was scheduled for 8.30 p.m. I waited until about seven-thirty and then I started to get ready.

When it was about eight o'clock, I was ready and my aunt noticed and said, 'Who you'll be getting to go down with you?'

'Nobody. Not a single soul. I mean, if I see someone going down there it's all right. I'll have company. But if not, I'll just take a cool walk down.'

My aunt came and stood up before me. She said firmly, 'I orready tell you that you mustn't walk by yourself on that beach road. Especially when the night black like pitch, like tonight. You keep saying you don't believe, but ah telling you, boy, *it have soucouyant.*'

She sat down there, the finger pointing at me, admonishing me. I wanted to laugh at how she could be so serious about this nonsense, and at the same time I wanted to laugh at the way she herself looked. Her head was tied with a check scarf and her eyes were red and watery, with the edge of the eyelids turned up. Her nose was like a hawk's and as she talked it bobbed up and down. And as for talking, that was another story: when she talked, her mouth was something to see, for it was bare of teeth, with the gums pink and the tongue red. Really, my old aunt should never talk about soucouyant. Because she looked exactly like a witch —

in fact she looked exactly how a soucouyant should look!

She said, 'Oh, you laughing? You think they does teach everything in college? Ha!'

I remained silent. As I buttoned up my shirt-sleeves, I thought of saying something to my aunt, but I was reluctant. For you could not change these elderly people. When they held on to a point they held on to it for life. Yet the very idea of soucouyant was so ridiculous that I could not help speaking. 'Tantie, I ain't arguing. Your belief is your belief. But the youngsters in this modern age can't believe in anything like soucouyant. That is superstition.'

She burst out laughing, her crinkled face showing up in the glare of the pitch-oil lamp. 'Superskission, Shiver me timbers! Superskission? Don't kill me! I done see soucouyant with me own two eyes and now this boy calling it superskission.' She laughed 'Heh, heh!' and then she turned to me and said seriously, 'That could *never* be superskission.'

I said nothing.

She said, 'You young people, you don't believe in nothing until you see something to frighten you. You going to a school concert that have singing and dancing on the stage, but everything in life ain't singing and dancing. Look, boy, listen, eh! Listen, to what I have to tell you: *life have evil.*'

'I know life have evil.'

I left her and I went and put on my tie and in a few moments I was ready to go. Besides, I was already fed up. I thought of something and I knew this was the only thing to keep my aunt quiet. I went and said to her, 'Okay, Tantie, you said you see soucouyant orready with your own two eyes. Now tell me what a soucouyant look like.'

She laughed, 'Ha! Ha!' And her high-pitched voice seemed to be tossed about on the breeze. She said, 'Everything good to eat but not everything good to talk. But I'll tell you — a soucouyant is a thing that does deal with the devil. Human being in the day and devil in the night. It does fly and it does suck blood. Evil, evil. She does look like this and she does do that . . .'

My aunt was making actions to show me and what she was doing really looked ugly and awful. She continued, still making actions, 'And they does do so and so. And they does jump so. And they does wear ah old dress looking like a sack. And they does take off their skin, and . . . Look, boy, that is Lucifer heself — though she's ah old lady. And you cyan't talk about shape, 'cause soucouyant always changing shape. Sometimes a soucouyant does open out like this, and sometimes a soucouyant does spin round like this, and sometimes is just a ball ah fire. Boy, if this kind ah thing meet you up in the road one night — ah telling you, run, yes!'

The way Tantie said, 'Run, yes!' sent shivers down my spine. She appeared to believe deeply in soucouyants, and the way she had been jumping about, and spinning around made it look as if these spooky witches really existed. That is, if you believed in that sort of thing. Yet for some odd reason, although I did not believe, I was not so anxious now to go out alone into this pitch-black night!

Tantie saw my reluctance and she said, 'Well you orready dress up, and it getting late, so you better go.'

'Tantie, it really blowing cold here on the beach. Perhaps I should pass round by Quarters.'

'Now? You'll reach in time? What's the time now?'

'A little past eight.'

'But if you go round Quarters now you'll be too late.'

'Oh well — perhaps.'

'Better to go on the beach road, man. Why not? You ain't 'fraid soucouyant!'

I looked down the beach and then I looked at her face. She said, 'I could reach you a little way. Up to the lagoon, if you like. But ah wouldn't cross Lagon Mahoe, you know. I cyan't promise you that.'

Her saying this got me even more scared, but I said, 'Okay, Tantie, let's go.'

She went inside and blew out the pitch-oil lamp, and then she came down the steps. The darkness was so dense I nearly walked into a coconut tree.

I cried, 'Tantie, where's you flambeau?'

'Here!' She struck a match and suddenly reddened the place. I winced and nearly fainted.

She did not notice and she went on whimpering in her whiny voice, 'Yes, as I was telling you. These people could be so evil.

When the time come for them to fly, they have to fly, but first they jump, you know, like this, and they put their skin . . .'

'All right, all right, Tantie. You have to talk about soucouyant now?'

'Oh, you 'fraid,' she said, and a weird peal of laughter rang through the night.

I did not say anything. An odd feeling had taken possession of me. I don't know if it was because of the presence of my old aunt, or whatever it was, but something made the night feel strange. Tantie herself made me feel scary when I looked at her by the light of the flambeau. Besides, although we were walking with the flambeau, I could see neither the beach nor the sea nor the coconut trunks. As we neared the lagoon Tantie began talking again, 'I ain't crossing that river. Not me. I ain't crossing Lagon Mahoe. I stopping right here. Take yuh time and go, eh! Sometimes it good to whistle a tune when you walking. I hope nothing ain't happen to you.'

'No, Tantie.' My jaws chattered. I was trembling, and it was not only because of the chilly wind.

My aunt said, 'You want me flambeau?'

'Yes, Tantie. But what about you?'

In the red light of the flambeau I could see her toothless smile. She said, 'You see, if I was a soucouyant now, I could fly back.' And she laughed.

I could not laugh. That was no kind of joke for Tantie to make. Especially as she looked a perfect one, with her red eyes, her pink gums, and her nose bobbing up and down.

'Tantie, I'll go with the flambeau.'

'Here, take it.'

As I stretched for it, it fell to the ground and went out. The place was so dark I could not see anything. I heard Tantie mumble, 'The damn thing will flare up now,' but I paid no mind to her, for my heart was thumping, and my hand was trembling like a leaf. There was the sound of fumbling on the sand and the sound of the scratch of a match but the next moment all I heard was 'voom!' and there was a big ball of fire in front of my face.

'Oh God!' I cried, and took off, running madly. I did not know if I was running towards the school, towards Plaisance, or towards the sea. Again and again I collided with coconut trees, fell down, got up, and began running again.

'Oh God!' I screamed once more, tears running down my face.

There was no noise except the low roar of the sea, and the noise of weird peals of laughter flaking off into the night.

3

How Mrs Feathery solved her problem

Mrs Feathery was the pleasant fat hen who lived at the top of the hill. She was a nice, quiet hen who always minded her own business, and she got along very well with the other animals: all except Mr Scaley, the snake; and Mr Hawk, the chicken-hawk.

Not that these two gentlemen kept themselves to themselves. They liked Mrs Feathery very much but she did not like them. In fact, she hated them and spent many nights up in her roost thinking how best to be rid of them. For they gave her a lot of pain. It did not matter where she laid her eggs, Mr Scaley would seek them out and would not rest until he found them. And he would proceed to devour them, because eggs were his passion.

But Mr Scaley did not always find them. There were times when he looked and looked and found nothing. At such times Mrs Feathery would be able to sit on her eggs for twenty-one days until she began to hear the little cheep-cheeps beneath her, which would overwhelm her with joy.

But what happened after a few days of walking around with her chicks? She gave a cluck of grief and a tear-drop fell to the ground. What would happen was that Mr Hawk would swoop down and carry off her chicks, one by one.

One day, as she was brooding over the problem, she became so distressed that her little shining eyes became red, and tears rolled down her beak. She thought, 'What shall I do? Something has to be done, but what shall I do?'

And suddenly a bright idea flashed across her mind. The more she thought of it, the more she liked it and, although the tears were still falling, she was anxious to put the idea into practice.

She said to herself, 'It is the best plan. I hope it will work.'

She thought about Mr Scaley and Mr Hawk, two good pals who always stuck together because they had the same awful habit. If her plan worked, what a wonderful world it would be! She would be able to lay and hatch her eggs in peace and to bring up her offspring just like anybody else.

That evening Mrs Feathery went for a walk. She went on purpose in the direction of the old poui tree and when she reached it she looked up quickly, then turned her head straight. Yes, sure enough, Mr Scaley was at home. He was up there, coiled around a branch, and his head was pushed cosily under where his tail curled round, and his eyes were like two bright diamonds in his little head.

Mrs Feathery was passing straight but she was not walking briskly now — she had checked her speed. Mr Scaley watched for a little while but he thought he would not say anything because he felt she was looking for a place to lay, and he wanted to see. But when she turned back and was passing under the tree again he called out, 'Oh, Mrs Feathery, you are taking a nice little evening walk?'

Mrs Feathery pretended she was taken aback. 'Cluck! Cluck! Mr Scaley, is that you? Just fancy! I am passing under your house without realising it is here you live. How are you?'

'I'm not so well,' said Mr Scaley. He said it very slowly and he bobbed his little head up and down, looking at Mrs Feathery to see if he could tell whether it was her laying time. He said, 'I am not feeling so well.' He was going to add, 'I need a little nourishment,' but he did not say that. That might send the heat to Mrs Feathery's head and set them quarrelling again. He respected Mrs Feathery's tongue. He simply said, 'I'm not so well; I'm taking a little rest.'

'Yes, you look a bit tired. Not anything as sprightly as our friend, Mr Hawk.'

Mr Scaley's eyes widened. *Our* friend, Mr Hawk! That was the last thing he expected Mrs Feathery to say, for it was only in the past week Mrs Feathery had given Mr Hawk a good tongue-lashing. He, Scaley, had coiled around a branch, completely hidden by the leaves, and he had heard the hen unleash such a torrent of abusive language against his friend that he had been shocked and bewildered. Not that Mr Hawk did not deserve it, though. He had just taken the last of Mrs Feathery's eight little chicks.

Now Mr Scaley chuckled and looked away, and then he said, 'How is he this morning? I mean our friend, Mr Hawk.'

'Oh, I've never seen him so chirpy. I met him by the old coconut tree stump where I went to look for wood-lice. He was telling me all about his friends. Oh, so funny!' Mrs Feathery was so convulsed in laughter that she almost got the hiccups.

'What did he say about me?' Mr Scaley asked anxiously. It was the sly way Mrs Feathery was laughing that caused him to ask that.

Mrs Feathery laughed even more, and now, after a bout of hiccups, she had to check herself. Then she said, 'Mr Scaley, please! Mr Hawk is my personal friend and I have no right telling you anything — even if what he said was unpleasant.'

Mr Scaley now sprang to life. He jerked his head backwards and his two bright eyes were glistening. 'Unpleasant? About me? That — that fellow doesn't know anything about me.' He had almost said 'that feathered fool,' but stopped just in time. He was looking Mrs Feathery straight in the face. 'What did Hawk say about me?'

'Cluck! Cluck!' Mrs Feathery said. 'Cool your temper, Mr Scaley, cool it. I never thought you were the type who got excited, otherwise I just wouldn't tell you anything. Even if he called you slippery and slimy, ignore him. Do like me. You know how many names they call me?'

'What!' Mr Scaley cried, 'He called me that?' The snake was enraged. His little beady eyes were now red, and his head was trembling. 'He called me that? Slippery and slimy? He'll know who's slippery and slimy!'

Mr Scaley began to hiss and uncoil himself hastily from the branch. Mrs Feathery had never seen him so flustered before and she tried to look worried but inside her she was rejoicing.

She said, 'You really stun me, Mr Scaley. After all, if I had only known, I would have gone my way straight. Mr Hawk was only making a joke, and if he said you were the biggest egg-thief, that isn't anything to get . . .'

Mr Scaley's sharp hiss startled Mrs Feathery. He exclaimed, 'He called *me* the biggest egg-thief? That shameless chicken-snatcher! That criminal! Let him call me that to me face and . . .' The snake slithered down the branch, then dropped suddenly to the ground.

Mrs Feathery cried, 'Good grief! Take it easy, Mr Scaley. Besides, Mr Hawk is not at home now. After he left me by the wood-lice nest, he said he was going down to the beach to see if he could get some fish.'

The snake stopped in his track and now he looked up at Mrs Feathery. 'Oh, it's fish now. It's fish now, not chicken.' He gave a derisive laugh and spat out, his forked tongue showing red.

Mrs Feathery said, 'He said he ain't eating chicken again.'

'No, he ain't eating chicken again because he's talking to chicken mother!'

'No it's not that. Ah . . . He said . . . Well I didn't want to tell you, but he said he had been keeping bad company.'

The snake jerked his head out, and the scales round his neck seemed to swell. 'Bad company? Aha! Oho! Well, he'll know what bad company give. It will be he and me down by the beach!'

As the snake said this, he threw himself into the bushes, while Mrs Feathery kept pleading, 'No, no! No, Mr Scaley, no!' She even dropped a tear and feigned distress.

Not only was Mr Hawk at home, but he was already in bed. He had done a lot of scouting around for chickens today and he was tired. In fact, although it wasn't dark yet, where he lay now he was good for the night. He had no plans to go a single place else, let alone to the beach. In any case, he never went to the beach in search of food, because life had not yet become *that* difficult. There were still a few chicken-coops around, and wherever there were chicken-coops there would be chicks.

As he thought 'chicks' he started, jerking himself up. For he was sure he had heard a chirp. Not a cheep, but a chirp. As if someone was calling. Some bird. He looked up, then down, but he saw no one. He settled down again. But just as his thoughts began to wander, once more the sound came loud and clear.

He looked right beneath him to the root of the immortelle tree and he made a squawk of surprise, 'Mrs Feathery, it is you?'

Mrs Feathery was serious. Her head was up, but her eyes were looking down at her beak. 'Mr Hawk, I am sorry to disturb you.'

'Oh, not at all. Oh, that's all right, Mrs Feathery. It is such a pleasure to see you. In fact, I was just thinking — I was just thinking all sorts of things.' He did not dare say he was thinking of chickens, although he always spoke the truth. He continued, 'I was thinking of all sorts of things, which brought you to mind. How are you?'

Mrs Feathery was looking away while Mr Hawk was talking. She was pretending to pay him no mind at all. Now that he had finished, she said stiffly, 'Mr Hawk, I know we don't always see eye to eye, but I wouldn't side with any animal against you. If I hear any animal speaking ill of you, I have to come here and tell you.'

'Speaking ill of me?' Mr Hawk said. 'Who will want to speak ill of me? I don't trouble nobody.' He was looking Mrs Feathery in the eye but she shifted her gaze as she was too embarrassed to face him.

He continued in innocent wonder, 'Who in the world will want to speak ill of someone who's so nice and . . .'

Mrs Feathery found this too much, and she cut in, 'Anyway, whatever quarrel we have between us, we are we – you know what I mean – and if I hear any animal calling you a dirty thief, it's bound to hurt me.'

'Me? A dirty thief?' Mr Hawk got enraged. He flapped his wings, turned round on the branch, then flew down onto the sand. He went and stood up right in front of Mrs Feathery. 'Who called me a dirty thief?'

'Mr Hawk, I can't tell you.'

'Come out with it. You said, "We is we." Don't bother about who is weevil. Come on! Who called me a dirty thief?'

'I can't . . .'

'Tell me!' he shrieked. 'Talk out.' He pecked hard at the immortelle root to sharpen his beak. Then he made three jumps and he shrieked so loudly Mrs Feathery pretended she took fright. He cried, 'Tell me!'

'I'm not going to call any names but it's a good friend of yours.'

'The only good friend I have is Mr Scaley and *he* wouldn't say that.'

Mrs Feathery gave a little mocking laugh. She said, 'I'm not calling names but he's a bosom friend.'

'The only bosom friend I have is Mr Scaley.'

'Mr Hawk, you want me to call names but I'm not calling any names. All I'll say is that it's a long, long friend of yours.'

The chicken-hawk jumped and then flew up to his branch again and then he flew back again to the ground. He was nervous and extremely irritated. In fact he was furious — so furious that it appeared as if he had lost his mind. He spun round and he gave three sharp pecks at the immortelle roots, and then he passed both sides of his beak on his wings to test the sharpness.

Then he gave a huge leap, flapping his wings.

And then he squeaked, almost croaked, 'The only long, long friend I have is Mr Scaley and I'm going down now to the poui tree for him to tell me who is the dirty thief.'

Mrs Feathery put on a look of shock. She cried, 'What's this, Mr Hawk? Do you mean you will fight with your good friend?'

'Good friend? That slippery, slimy, crawling. scaley good-for-nothing! Let me catch up with him. I'll tear him to shreds!'

Mrs Feathery said, 'Well, Cousin Hawk, as I said, you won't catch up with him on the poui tree. Because, as I was coming here, he was just going down to the beach. Fortunately.'

'Fortunately? I'm going right down to the beach to meet him. Right now.' And so saying, the chicken-hawk flapped his wings and flew up into the air, spun around, and disappeared behind the trees.

It was not long afterwards that Mrs Feathery, hiding in the clump of bushes next to the beach, heard the terrible battle between Mr Scaley and Mr Hawk. They fought all morning and Mrs Feathery at times had a view of the battle, and at other times just heard the flapping, fluttering wings, amidst the swishing of the long tail, and the hissing and the scraping of claws.

When at last the fight was over, and both Mr Scaley and Mr Hawk lay on the sand, weak and panting for breath, Mrs Feathery ran away to her little home on the hill. She hurried to her nest, as it was her laying time, and she laid the egg, confident now that it would not be troubled. And afterwards, when she turned round to look at it, she cackled with laughter at the snake and the chicken-hawk, her arch enemies.

As the days went by, she laid several more eggs, and when they were hatched she told the story to all the little chickens. And in fact, from that day, when hens lay they always cackle with laughter because they remember the trick Mrs Feathery played on the two thieves.

4

The dog who came to the city

The dog, Pablo, decided to leave Maraval and he went and told the old lady. She was surprised. She said, 'I've always treated you well. The only thing I couldn't do was to take you for walks. It's okay for Philip. Philip is young. I am an old lady. In any case, you prefer Philip. But how you'll get to Woodbrook? I mean, you can't pass through the town — you ain't know the town.'

Pablo, in his own language, retorted, 'That's what you always say. I can't pass through the town. I *will* pass through the town. If Philip will not come, something is wrong. I will go to him.'

'Have some patience, Pabs. Give him a chance, he just got married. After all! Maybe something's keeping him. But he'll come. I don't like the idea of you going down to Woodbrook. I mean, just imagine a dog crossing through Port-of-Spain. It have so many cars and trucks and buses, you'll sure get crushed. Because you don't know how to go. The main trouble is that some of the streets are one-way and all over have traffic. Dogs can't read. You won't know what street to take. You won't reach, Pablo!' The old lady looked very worried.

'I will reach,' Pablo said. 'I will reach, all right.' He was speaking in dog language, which the old lady understood. 'I will reach,' he said again. And as he thought of Philip, he whined and wagged his tail, and a bead of tear rolled down on each side of his face.

The old lady felt distressed, and that evening, when she

reckoned that Philip had arrived home from work, she telephoned him. She just dialled the number and waited.

'Hello,' Philip's voice answered.

'Philip, it's me.'

'You aren't on about that dog again!' he said. He made a long 'stupes' but his heart bled.

'Yes, I'm on about that dog, but don't forget it's your dog. Philip, I don't believe in cruelty to animals. The dog hardly eating since you left, and it's weeks now you get married. Boy, the dog missing you. I can't take him for walks and I can't make as much of him as you do.' She paused and Philip said nothing.

'Look, Phil, try and come and take the dog. Try and make Cynthia understand and please come for Pablo. Else he'd try to come for himself, you know. And then you know what will happen! If it's not a car it will be a truck, and if it's not a truck it will be a bus. But it will sure happen. And I'll tell you what, that dog is determined to come.'

'He told you so?' the son sneered. 'You was talking to Pablo again? No, tell me. Tell me you had a conversation with him and he said he was coming to look for me. Tell me good, Ma. Tell me, because dogs could talk!' Then he said, 'Every night now you ringing me to tell me about this dog.'

His mother said, 'I'm only telling you how he is these days. The dog is yours. It grieving. I ain't tell you a single thing about talking now. You feel it's a big joke. You keep on singing a song: "Dogs can't talk, dogs can't talk." If I say that Pablo and me does talk, that is a big joke for you. Okay, go on, laugh ha, ha, ha! What I'm telling you now is, try and get Cynthia to understand. The dog is grieving. The dog feeling pain. If I tell you Pablo was crying this morning you'll laugh too. Okay, all right. Me and me nonsense. All right. The point is, you know how he like to go with you for walks in the bush and thing. You can't only take Cynthia for walks, you know. In any case, Pablo want to live over by you. He want to be with you, not with me. Philip, you try and come and take the dog, for Heaven sake, you hear?'

Philip stood there and it tore his heart to hear that Pablo was grieving. But he said firmly, 'Ma, Woodbrook ain't have place to mind dogs.'

His mother never understood this sort of thing and this got her wild. She exclaimed, 'But Woodbrook *must* have place to keep dog. Ay, ay! What is Port-of-Spain coming to! You have people worse than dog living in Woodbrook. So look, you Mr Philip, you stop that nonsense, eh! So what you want to say, dog is not . . .' And she stopped. She was going to ask, 'Dog is not people too?' But she stuttered and said, 'Pablo is a nice dog, and you always giving him a bath. Ay, ay! My God, what I hearing today! You telling me it ain't have no place in Woodbrook for dogs. But dog is . . .' She stopped again. She was going to say, 'But dog is human.' She was so flustered and confused she did not know what to do next. She simply slammed down the telephone.

Cynthia happened to be standing a little distance from Philip, half-hiding behind the curtain. Now, seeing the expression on Philip's face, she said, 'What happen?'

'The line cut off.'

'She dashed down the phone!'

'Oh no,' Philip smiled nervously. 'It just cut off just like that. You know what these telephones give.'

'And why you jumped? If the line just cut off just so, why you jumped?'

'Ah, well . . .' Philip tried to turn off the conversation but Cynthia was tense now, and she knew exactly what was going on. She came and laid her hand on his shoulder and she said, 'Well, listen eh, and this is for your information. You ain't married that dog, you married me. And I already tell you I don't want any damn dog in this house. We married seventeen days now and every day I only hearing about dog, dog, dog. I ain't want any dog in this yard. Besides, where you'll keep dogs in Woodbrook?'

Philip swung round. 'Where you'll keep dogs in Woodbrook? Girl, don't make me laugh. It have people worse than dog living in Woodbrook. I only tell Ma you can't keep dogs in Woodbrook because of you. Because of the way you hate Pablo.'

She was taken aback to see him flare up. She said, 'Hate Pablo? I don't hate Pablo. But the way you keep on talking about him seems he must be some God or something. I see you was trying to shout down your own Ma because she was saying the dog could talk, but all the time we was courting, didn't you yourself use to tell me Pablo does talk to you? You see, you are a damn liar too. But anyway, I want to say this. Get this clear. The day you bring that dog here — the day Pablo walk in, I walk out.' And with that she swung round and stamped out of the dining-room.

Philip stood there and his heart burned. What must he do now? What *could* he do! What should he do? The only three persons he loved in this world were his mother, Cynthia, and Pablo. Yes, Pablo was a person too. His mother had nearly said Pablo was human but Pablo wasn't *nearly* human, he was human. More human than a lot of people he, Philip, knew.

He took off his spectacles and wiped his red eyes. Cynthia did not understand this but Pablo was 'people.' He had never yet met another dog who could talk — or perhaps the better way to put it was to say that he had never yet met a dog whose language he could understand. Yet if he told anybody in the world about Pablo, anybody except his mother, he would be jeered and laughed at.

And one thing he never knew, he never knew that his mother was in possession of the secret. How was it possible? He was jealous, in a way. For he had learned to understand Pablo's language through love, and through, he liked to think, through what he had put into the sugar-water he had fed the dog as a pup.

There was really no reason for his thinking this way. Only that from the day he had given that drink to Pablo he began to understand every word that Pablo said. And he had given that drink to the pup because he had seen his mother do it. But, apart from the sugar-water, he slept and woke with dog language on his mind. And, most embarrassing of all, sometimes he forgot and spoke dog language to people too! And then there was Cynthia, who Pablo knew only very slightly. In fact, Pablo had taken it well when he heard about the marriage, and when he saw the girl he had just accepted her. He accepted her with silence, it was true, but he had still accepted her. And on the wedding day, when Philip had gone out to the back landing with a drink of whisky in his hands, Pablo had come up the back steps and said, 'So, Philip, I hear you ain't taking me with you?'

Philip had replied in the same language, 'But of course, Pablo. Of course you coming. But you'll have to wait a little. Till we settle down, you know what I mean. You got the heap of bones I fixed up for you?'

The dog had nodded.

'Well, look,' Philip had said, 'It doesn't matter about any friend I have. You are my best friend. We know what we know. Today you outside and other people inside but I prefer you any day. If you come inside they'll say this and they'll say that, but this is your house. This morning, when I was chatting with the best-man, he said, 'I never see dog in wedding,' and that's why you ain't inside. But in any case you know what you-know-who would say. But Pablo, a wedding is just one day. It ain't nothing. Listen, Pablo, I

want you in the new place in Woodbrook. I want you there. Just give me a little chance to settle down over there and then I'll come for you.'

But now Philip had to face the reality of the moment. How could he take Pablo there when Cynthia was so jealous of the dog? How could he do that without breaking up his marriage? For days now he had wanted to go over to Maraval to see Pablo but how could he face Pablo and tell him that Cynthia did not even want him in the yard, let alone in the house? His eyes filled up with water and the world seemed to swim around him. His mother had said that since he had left, Pablo had hardly eaten. What could he, Philip, do? Hot tears rolled down his cheeks and he took out his handkerchief again.

Cynthia was standing at the kitchen door, watching. She came up to him now with her arms akimbo. Her face bore the expression of shock and disbelief, and she stared him in the face. 'Oh-h,' she said. 'Oh.' And she nodded her head slowly. Then she said, 'I'm so sorry, Philip, I've only just realised what the situation is. It's not me you want in this house,' she said, her voice getting louder. 'It's not *me*, it's that dog. It's that Pablo. Well, okay. I'll clear out of your house now for now.' And she dashed hysterically into the bedroom and slammed the door.

'No, no,' Philip dashed after her. 'No, Cynthie, oh God, don't let's break up like that!' He grabbed her by a sleeve.

'Leave me alone,' she cried, opening the wardrobe and throwing clothes on the bed.

'Please don't go, Cynthie, please.'

She had a cluster of clothes under her arm and she was going to put the bundle in a bag, but as he kept on pleading she turned around to him and said, 'Look, Philip, I'm sick and tired of this nonsense. I can't take no more of this. I'm giving you the last, last chance. If you ever mention the word "Pablo" ever again in your whole life, I ain't saying nothing more. But I know when you come home from work you ain't seeing me!'

At Maraval, some evenings afterwards, Pablo came to a decision. After pining for Philip so much, and after feeling tired of waiting for him to come, he went up to the old lady.

He said in his own language, 'I can't wait no more. I'm going to Woodbrook. You said I won't reach, but I'll reach. Tell me how to go and I will reach.'

The old lady said, 'Like you'll really have to go. You have to go, in truth. You think you'll make it? Port-of-Spain is no joke, you know. Hm! With that traffic. I don't know why Philip don't come for you, believe me.'

'You said to give him a chance but it's days and days now. Philip must be busy.'

'Yes, I say so too. Because he should be settled down already. Because he married since the 20th of June.'

Pablo whined something to the old lady and she replied, 'No, not really. It depends on who it is. And who your wife is. Sometimes people does take a long time to settle down, and sometimes again it's quick.' Then she stopped and said, 'What's that? No I don't know much about Cynthia,' and she looked out of the window.

Then she said to herself, 'They hardening their heart against this dog!'

Pablo was still there, sitting, looking up at her, and she shook off those clawing thoughts and she said, 'Look, I'm not against your going, but the place hard to find. It's hard for people to find, much less for a dog, and if I . . .'

Pablo made a few yaps and she retorted, 'I know you have four legs and we have two, but that doesn't say nothing — I always tell you that you is a saucy dog! And stubborn. And you like too much back-chat.' Angrily, she glared at him and pointed a warning finger. Then she softened after a few moments. She said, 'Look, I have to tell you how to go, and listen to me good. Philip is in Carlos Street, Woodbrook, you hear that? Carlos Street, Woodbrook. You could read?'

And then she put both hands to her head and looked up to heaven for guidance. Dogs could not read, so what was the use of saying 'Carlos Street, Woodbrook?'

She said, 'Now listen good. Walk up this very road till you

45

come to the junction with Long Circular — but walk on the side, don't forget; keep on the pavement. Right?'

Pablo nodded his head.

The old lady went on, 'When you come to the Long Circular Road, turn left, and then walk on the right hand side.' Then she said sharply, 'Look, Pablo, I don't want to hear no more about what dogs does do. People prefer to walk on the right so they could see the traffic coming on their side, and I want you to do that too and get to Woodbrook. Walk on the right but don't follow nobody and don't keep too close to anybody. I'm telling you this because before you know anything they'll say you is their dog. Now when you walk a little way you'll see a gasoline station on the other side, and then not too far down you'll come to a next one . . .'

Pablo interrupted the old lady and she said, 'No, who told you that? That isn't far. It's far for me because I so old I have to walk slow, but that ain't really far. And especially for a dog — for a dog that ain't nothing. Okay, listen, from the gas station you continue – now you on the other side of the road – you continue and then you come to what people call "The Queen's Park Savannah". You know "The Queen's Park Savannah"?'

Pablo shook his head.

'Never mind, you'll come to it and it's so big and grassy, with tall trees, you can't mistake it for nothing else. Pablo, I said shut up! Lord, what sort of dog is this? Look, before you come to the Savannah you'll see a little roundabout. You could cross the road and walk down the pitch walk. It have some big houses on the other side, what they call the "Mag-" something or other. I getting so old I can't even remember. But . . .'

Pablo was looking at her but he was not seeing her. If he could only write, and could make notes! How could he remember all those details? He looked at her, then he looked to the ground, trying to commit all those fine details to memory.

The old lady noticed that his mind was wandering and she said sharply, 'Pablo, you listening? I want you to listen and listen good, because right now you'll have to be careful. Now if I was talking to people – if I was talking to a human being who could read – I could direct them easy, but anyway, listen and pay attention. Now after you cross, and you walking down the pitch-walk near those . . . those big houses, now you have yuh face towards the sea. When you get down to where the Savannah curve, it have a college on the other side and then a little roundabout. Don't curve with the road, but cross. When you cross, the road that going down straight is Maraval Road.'

Pablo nodded but he was bewildered. The old lady did not look at his eyes.

'Okay, you'll walk right down Maraval Road and the second big cross street with the lights is Ariapita Avenue. Take Ariapita Avenue and turn right. No. Let me see. No, turn left.' She rubbed her nose and then scratched her head. 'It's years I ain't go down Port-of-Spain but ah trying to tell you the easiest way because I know Woodbrook good. Yes, from Ariapita Avenue you'll turn right — I mean left — no, right. What happening to me at all? You'll turn right, and count one, two, three streets — you could count at all?'

Pablo lowered his head and said he could count only from one to five. The old lady laughed and said, 'But suppose it's more than five streets? This dog could kill me, yes! Anyway you want to get to Philip and I'll tell you how to get to Philip.'

She thought a little and a bright idea struck her. She said, 'Okay, don't bother. You don't have to count. Forget that. Now listen well. Walk until you come to a square, and take, not the second street —

now we talking about *after* the square. Not really after the square, but it's the street on the other side of the square. Let me see, it's Carlos, Alfredo and Alberto. Don't confuse youself, forget Alfredo and Alberto. It's Carlos Street you want. Sniff out the sea and go down Carlos Street, past the nice little church, and on the right hand side is Philip's house. The number is 35.'

Then she scratched her head and made 'stupes.' She said to herself, 'What's the use? He can't count. He don't know numbers.' There was a thoughtful pause and then she said, 'Well, anyway. Look out good, eh? Philip always say you are an intelligent dog. Shut up, you don't have to boast. Just listen! The house is on the right — no, on the left — just a minute. The house is on the right. Well, walk good and use yuh nose good to smell out Philip. He's always boasting about how you is a master smeller. Smell him out because he living right there. You don't have to count if you don't know figures. Use your nose good.'

And now she said slowly, using a warning finger, 'But don't go down to the end of that street, for God sake. At the end of that street is Wrightson Road. Don't go down there. You know what down there famous for? Well don't reach as far as Wrightson Road, for Heaven's holy sake. Else yuh coo-coo cook. Down there have dog-catchers.' She almost whispered the word, 'dog-catchers.' She looked him straight in the eye. 'Now you understand me good?'

Pablo looked away and did not answer. He wasn't going anywhere near Wrightson Road, she did not need to worry. All he was going to was number 35 and, although he could not count, he had got enough ideas from Philip to know all he had to look for was a 3 and a 5 together.

He was anxious to leave the presence of the old lady because he had several things in his head to remember and she herself was so mixed up he was afraid she would get him mixed up too. He could not afford to be mixed up now, and if his memory failed him at all he would either lose his way or be in the hands of the dog-catchers. He scampered off without even saying goodbye.

It was easy for Pablo to find the St Clair roundabout, and easier still to find Ariapita Avenue. But when he got to the junction of Ariapita Avenue, he stood up, dazed, because the maze of traffic and houses and people proved too much for him. A flash of memory came to him — a memory of long, long ago, when Philip had taken him as a pup to some man called Vet or something like that. The man had put something down his throat. He remembered this only vaguely, because it was so long ago. Anyway, the main thing now was to find this square. He could not remember whether the old lady had said turn right or left here, and in any case he did not know right from left. Why should he? When the old lady said 'It's on the left hand' it didn't affect him because he did not have any hand. He had found his way here because the old lady had said 'towards the sea,' and he could always sniff out the sea. Now, a little excited, he ran off to one side, and when he did not see the square he came back to the junction and stood up, and then he ran off to the other side. It was not long before he found a square in front of him and now his heart began to pound. When he came to the far end of the square, he stopped. Somehow he could not sniff the sea now because of the fumes of gasoline from the passing cars and he felt he would have to ask where the sea was because he could not remember if the old lady had said right or left or in front of him. There were a lot of people but he could not ask, because as a rule people could not understand dog language. He had seen several dogs but, looking around, he could not see any now, but he saw a gate with the words 'Beware of the Dog.'

He knew that because of Philip. As a rule Philip showed him those signs when they went for walks, and he could easily read the word 'dog' because Philip had spent several hours teaching him that. But in spite of Philip's effort he always spelt 'DOG' backwards, 'GOD'. This amused Philip no end and Philip always laughed, but still Pablo saw it as the word for 'dog.' He sat down in front of that gate and yapped.

When the dog came out, Pablo asked where Philip lived and the dog did not know. Then Pablo asked where the sea was and the dog pointed a paw. Pablo asked, 'On the right or on the left?'

When he saw his companion was puzzled, he affected surprise. He said, 'You don't know right from left?' And then he informed the dog, 'It is either on this side or on that side,' and he trotted off down the road.

But it was now that he began feeling troubled. The further down he went, the more uncertain he felt. He was walking now and keeping his nose to the ground to see if he could smell Philip, and at the same time he was glancing in at the houses on either side of the street to see if he could spot him. He could not remember all the fine details that the old lady had given him, but Number 35 kept ringing in his head. Number 35. He could only count up to five, but he knew a three and he knew a five. He kept looking around, but he could not see Philip. On one occasion he heard talking in a house and he stood up and flapped his long ears. But it was not Philip. He walked a little with his nose to the ground, then he stood up and looked back at the houses he had passed and at the houses that were beside him and at the houses that were in front, but still there was no sign of Philip. Once, with his nose to the ground he thought he smelled Philip and he spun round excitedly, but the smell was gone. And he did not know if it was a whiff of Philip he had had or if it was just the memory of other times that was playing a trick with him. His eyes were full of water as he walked down the street.

The young woman stood in a corner of the verandah and watched the big brown-and-white dog pass, and she laughed softly to herself.

In front of her were hanging baskets of fern, and at her back, open to view, were the huge silvery letters: NUMBER 35.

She had had a good description of the dog, and now, keeping well behind the flower baskets, she watched.

Nothing amused her so much as watching the antics of this dog. She watched him walk with his nose to the ground, then trot, then stop and look back as if bewildered, then stare about him on either side, then trot again, then stop and spin round as if he was crazed by some scent or something, then walk on, staring about and whining. She had chuckled until she could not help herself. Then she laughed even more heartily, though softly, as he passed the house going down the road. She was so happy that she leaned up, watching.

Pablo had nearly reached the junction of Carlos Street and Wrightson Road when he saw a man smiling at him. First, the gentleman had whistled and made a sign beckoning to him. He looked at the gentleman and the gentleman called out, 'Is all right, you could talk — I does talk dog language. Nobody ain't bound to know what we saying.'

Pablo first wanted to ask if there were any dog-catchers about, because he felt the cross-street in front *had* to be Wrightson Road. But as the street looked clear he went up to the man.

He whined plaintively, 'You could help me find Number 35?'

'You know numbers?' the man asked, looking a little agitated, 'You could count?'

'Only up to five.'

'Well start from this end,' said the man, 'and count five, and then another five, and then another five.' The man was grinning nervously now. He removed one hand from behind his back to show Pablo how to count.

'You know right from left? Because you have this side and that side. Look, you have to count like this: watch me hand. On this side one, on that side two, on this side three, on that side four . . .'

Pablo was sitting on his tail, right up in front of the man, near Wrightson Road, and as the man moved his hand and flicked his fingers towards the houses on either side, so Pablo's head moved to either side until he was giddy and mesmerised.

Then, with the hand that was behind his back, the dog-catcher simply threw the net around the brown-and-white dog. But as he swung to fling Pablo into the van, a scream rang out and a woman ran into the road.

The dog-catcher stood up as if seized.

'Mister, not that dog,' Cynthia cried. 'That is the only thing I can't take. I don't like dog, but anything worse than dog is catching dog.'

'This is your dog?' the disappointed dog-catcher asked.

'Yes, how you mean? This is our dog. The name is Pablo.'

Pablo wagged his tail, and the man said to the lady, 'That's true. Okay, take him. Is me first for the day, but take him.'

Cynthia untangled Pablo from the net and took him up the steps of Number 35.

5

In the bushes near the school

The boy in the broad-brimmed hat playfully grabbed the bell and dashed into the bushes, laughing. The whole band of children ran off after him and it was the noises and shrieks that attracted the teacher. She was standing on the steps of the school-house and watching. She had always told the children not to go into the bushes, for she did not want to be responsible for any snake-bites, or for any stings or torn dresses, or stained shirts or for any scratches or bruises.

Nor indeed for any lost child! She shuddered at the thought. The children's voices were dying away now and, as she thought this last thought, she hastened to the table and rang the bell as loudly as she could. Then she went back and stood up on the steps.

The shrill little voices, which had almost faded completely, began waxing louder and louder again, and in a short while the children burst excitedly into the school-yard. The teacher breathed a sigh of relief. She said, 'Thank God!'

All the children rushed back into their class-rooms. All, that is, except one — the one in the broad-brimmed hat. He sat on a tree-stump and was beckoning one of the little boys to come out and play with him.

The little boy slipped out and met him in the bushes and said hastily, 'School call. You didn't hear the bell? Hurry up, you ain't coming? I have to go back.'

As he turned to go, the one in the broad-brimmed hat tugged at his shirt-sleeves, and he turned back to see the tearful face, the pleading eyes.

'Why you crying?'

The tearful boy stuttered, 'I . . . want to . . . to play a little . . . bit.'

'But school call. You didn't hear school call?'

The tearful boy formed words which his companion was hardly able to hear.

'What you say? What's my name? It's Neville. But I can't stay to play, you know. We have to go inside. What class you in?'

As he spoke, there was another clang of the school-bell, and he looked around and said, 'Let's go now. We'll be late.' As he said this, he dashed away. But he went alone into the school.

When he arrived in class the teacher was just about to report, 'One missing.' She grabbed him and said, 'I knew it was you. You always give me the creeps. Didn't I say not to go into the bushes?'

'It's me friend.'

'Which friend?' the teacher said, looking across the class.

'He ain't here.'

'He isn't — why?'

One of the little girls said, 'No, Miss. He ain't in this class.' The child looked around the school-house. 'He ain't come back in school, Miss. He was wearing a hat like this, with a broad rim.' She had touched her hat, and she was now showing with her hands how broad the brim was. She continued, 'And he have vine and bush coming down from the hat like this. And he small like this.'

The teacher laughed heartily at the way the child was showing how the little fellow was. Then she said, 'But child you're talking about a douen! Broad-brimmed hat with vine and bush growing on it!' Then she laughed so heartily that she nearly choked.

But the children grew frightened, and the same little girl who had spoken, said, 'A douen, Miss?'

'Yes,' the teacher said, 'Don't you know what a douen is? Well I'll tell you, because you might meet one up one day.' And seeing the fright on the children's faces, she laughed again. Then she said, 'You children must learn our folklore. Douens are supposed to be little creatures of the forest. They are said to be children who died before they were christened. And their souls cannot rest. That's why they have to wander in the forests forever. They have their little feet turned back-to-front so when you follow them you can't come back.' She paused and laughed. Then she said, warningly, 'When they take other little children into the forest, you never see these children again.'

Everyone was silent, and the teacher cried, 'Come on, class. Don't be sad. It's only our folklore! I'll draw you a douen on the blackboard.'

When the teacher had finished drawing the douen, it looked so funny that all the children laughed, and when she went to rub it off, some of them begged her please to leave it because they wanted to copy it. And then, after they had finished, she rubbed it off and they passed on to their real lesson.

But Neville sat there dumb-struck. He could not get the drawing out of his mind. The picture the teacher drew on the blackboard was so much like his little friend that he could not believe. Although the drawing had been rubbed off the blackboard, he could still see the little fellow seated on the tree-stump, and he could not take his mind off his friend. He said to himself, 'Tomorrow I'll look for him, the little scamp!'

Next day, when the boys were playing 'Police and Thief' in the school-yard, Neville, who was the 'policeman,' saw one of the 'thieves' dash into the bushes. He plunged into the bushes after him, and after chasing him for some time he discovered that he was running after his friend of the previous day. He kept on chasing, having to jump over drains and run around trees, and

through thickets, and although he realised that both himself and his friend were tired, neither of them would give up. He himself was panting and he wanted to give up, but he could not face up to it. The Police never gave up. He had to pursue until he dropped. He followed his weakening friend far into the high woods until, at long last, the friend faltered and fell and Neville pounced on him.

Neville said, 'I arrest you . . . in the name . . . of the law.' He was blowing so hard that he had to hold his waist and pause a little.

His companion looked up at him and beamed. He was far from being sad-faced now, and what was strange, he was not even perspiring.

'Back . . . to . . . the jail-yard,' Neville said.

The boy with the broad-brimmed hat let Neville push and pull him about without their getting very far out of the forest. Neville began to be a little concerned about getting out, and now he was suddenly alarmed because he thought he heard the school-bell. He was not sure. There was a faint sound. At this moment he forgot he was supposed to be a policeman.

'School call. Let's go.'

His companion said nothing but looked away into the forest.

'Come. Let's go. You ain't hear the bell? I ain't arrest you again. Let's go before Teacher get the creeps.'

Instead of answering him, the little boy began to ramble amongst the trees, and then he seemed to pluck his broad-brimmed hat from amongst the branches, and then he went and sat on a tree-stump. Straightaway Neville began shaking, because he was recalling the picture the teacher had drawn on the blackboard. He looked at the deep dark forest around him and he cried, 'Oh, God! Tell me, little feller — you is not a douen? The teacher say you are a douen, she drew you on the blackboard yesterday.'

It was only now that he noticed the feet pointing the wrong way. He cried, 'Oh you is a douen in truth!'

He screamed with fright as the little boy rose from the tree-stump. The school itself was far away, and Neville was so weak and confused there was no way he could get out of the forest.

6

The night of Papa Bois

Papa Bois sat on a big vine that was running across the entrance of the forest. With him were three of his neighbours: Lappe, Tatou, and Monkey. They stayed there on guard, for they were expecting huntsmen to come into the forest, and as they waited, they talked about how best they could outwit these people.

Tatou, who was nervous, said, 'When you see them, plunge into the water.' That was the way *he* always escaped the gun of the hunter. But he did not realise that not all the animals could do as he did. Papa Bois listened to him and smiled.

The old man now looked at the lappe to see what sort of advice he had to give. The lappe said, 'It is better to go down into a hole. There you do not get wet.'

Papa Bois laughed so much he could hardly contain himself. Was it because the lappe lived in a hole? He turned around to the monkey. 'And what says my good friend?'

The monkey did not laugh. He remained still, his ears pricked. He was sure he could hear a sound like the breaking of brambles in the near distance. He was not too far from the balata tree and he was ready to dash off to it at any moment. As he looked at Papa Bois and saw the grey, flowing beard and the human face, the hairy human chest, and the human legs, he wondered how long this old man would side with them against the hunters. For although Papa Bois sometimes turned into lappe, and deer, and even monkey, when he turned back into human form he was really human — like the hunters. One day he was bound to give them up, and that day might be now. The monkey was a little distrustful and afraid, although this old man had been a friend of the whole forest.

The monkey again heard sounds, this time like people talking, and he turned around nervously to the lappe and the tatou. They were both trembling. He looked at Papa Bois, who was reeling out coils of thick vine about him. Papa Bois was going to speak, but the voices burst upon them and when he looked about him he was alone. For in a flash the tatou, the lappe, and the monkey had all scampered away. The only other sound that came to him, apart from the hunters' boots and the hunters' voices, was the loud splash of the tatou in the nearby river.

The hunters came upon Papa Bois, who was now sitting on a tree-trunk. They were taken aback to meet an old man in the forest, and they said, 'Old man, what you doing — hunting?'

'Yes.' The old man was holding an object shaped exactly like a gun.

They asked, 'You kill anything yet?'

'Not yet. The dogs just went so.' He pointed to one side of the high woods.

'We want to get over this way. Over there. By a balata tree. We hear that underneath does have plenty lappe. And sometimes you does even get monkey. Monkey love balata so bad, they does live on the balata tree.'

The second hunter said, 'Monkey love balata and I love monkey. Oh, God! I don't know how monkey meat sweet so!'

Papa Bois pointed to the other side, 'That is the way to the balata tree. Take this little track.'

The first hunter asked, 'Balata in season?'

Papa Bois replied, 'And monkey too. Pass this way. Go so.'

The forest track opened out wide and clear before the two hunters, and in their anxiety they rushed ahead of the old man. At a certain point they glanced back and, not seeing him, they assumed he could not move on fast, being so aged, and so they had left him behind.

They hurried forward and — crash! The first hunter tripped over a vine and fell. The other close behind tumbled over him and the gun he was holding nearly went off.

'Oh, blazes!' the one on top said.

As they were getting up, a deer broke into the track and ran ahead of them. They scrambled to their feet and gave chase desperately. The deer bounded over a liane but neither hunter had seen this vine and they tripped again, tumbling heavily to the ground.

The hunter who was behind said, 'Oh, God! You have to look out for these vines. What happen to you, man?' He was sprawled out, and the liane was entangled about his feet. The other was puffing so heavily he could hardly speak.

After a few moments they rose up weakly, and they stood looking in the direction in which the deer had gone. It was useless to give chase now. In any case, they did not have the strength. The first hunter was still panting, and as he turned around he saw a big manicou, the eyes glistening, from a nearby chenet tree.

As he turned to talk about it, a lappe bounded across the path. It was so sudden that they were dazed for a moment, and then they dashed into the bushes after it. The moon was bright and as they ran and stumbled and tripped and fell and ran again they could see the lappe big before their eyes.

They could have easily shot it, but they would have had to stand up to aim, and then they might have lost the lappe altogether. But they did not give up the chase. They were only hoping to get close enough to knock down the beast with the butt of the gun.

But chasing the lappe, tripping over vines and falling, stumbling over banks, having to jump over streams, and often bouncing up against trees — these things made them so weak and tired they felt they could chase no more. And in any case, they could not now see to continue, because the bright moon had faded out of the sky. Now the night was black. The breeze was

beginning to blow cold and at the moment all they could hear was a monkey chattering in the tree above them.

The second hunter, who had said he liked monkey meat, did not bother to think of the monkey at this moment because his mind was crazed with wondering how to get out. For they had run so much, and in all sorts of circles and zig-zags, that they had no idea in what part of the forest they were now. Neither of them had any idea where to turn — whether to go to the east, or west, or north or south. And they could not seek the old man's help because they had no idea where to find him. Still, not knowing whether he was near or far, they did try calling out to him, but only their echoes answered them. Their echoes and the dismal forest.

Now they sat down on the ground and the first hunter felt so exhausted his eyes were closing down with sleep. He said, 'It look as if we properly lost now. It ain't have nothing more we could do.'

His companion was bewildered. He did not know if he should scream or cry.

The first hunter whispered, 'I can't keep up no more. I have to get some sleep. The best thing is to lie down right here. Thank goodness Trinidad ain't have any animals what in love with human meat. Let's sleep and we'll see what we could do in the morning.'

Next morning, at the rising of the sun, the first hunter got up and roused his companion. His companion opened his eyes and jumped up to his feet. He said, 'We have to find a way to get outa here. Don't know if the old man spread the alarm — in any case, he couldn't know we got lost . We . . .' then he stopped. He said, 'Why you laughing? You find out how we could get out?'

'Yes,' the first hunter said. And he smiled, half-ashamed, and shook his head. 'Yes, I know how we'll get out.'

His friend said, 'You know where the old man is? He ain't gone home?'

'I don't know where the old man is but I know *who* he is. And that's why we'll get out.'

His friend was puzzled. 'Can't understand. How come? What you mean?'

'Well, it's only now the whole thing come to me. You remember all this vine we was tripping up with and falling down, and then the deer appear and then the lappe. And then you remember the monkey up in the tree and the manicou in the moonlight? Well, all this happen because we are hunters. Because the old man in the forest was the old man of the forest. You don't know about him? He's the friend of all the animals . . .'

His companion was shocked, 'Papa Bois? Is Papa Bois you talking about?'

'Yes. That was Papa Bois.'

'Christ!'

'Well, don't call Christ yet. Because it clear now what we have to do. Because all what happen last night was the work of Papa Bois. It's he who made us get properly lost and if the gun had gone off when ah fell down you'd be properly killed. And all that to protect the animals. Look, if you want to get out and get back home, do like me. Take off all your clothes and turn them inside out. And it wouldn't have any trouble again. Come, let's do that and let's go.'

It was bright morning when the two hunters climbed up the bank and into the main road. They were staggering with hunger and thirst and they were comical to look at with their trousers, shirts, and hats turned inside out. People just laughed.

As they tried to hurry to their homes, the second hunter said, 'Never me again. Never me again to hunt out of season.'

His companion turned to him, 'That's what they say. They say you mustn't hunt out of season. But I so scared I ain't going inside any forest any time again. I'm finished with hunting. You asking why? Because any season might be season for Papa Bois.'

7

The dancing lady

The lady with the flashy broad-brimmed hat attracted Phil's attention right away. It was a bluish hat trimmed with silk, and she was wearing a beautiful greenish velvety gown. It was odd, but no car had brought her, she had just walked in as if from the green forests just across the road. And she seemed so much at ease. The way she walked into the dance-hall one would have thought she belonged to this obscure village.

Phil turned to his friend Stanley, who was just beside him, 'Who is she, boy?'

Regarding this strange lady, Stanley was no wiser than Phil, but *his* heart, too, was racing. They looked at the slender figure, the stylish hat, and the velvety gown sweeping the floor. Phil said, 'In any case, wherever she come from, she's really glamorous. It's nice to see a star in this wilderness.'

Stanley didn't say anything but he was listening to his heart-beats. As he looked at every move the stranger made, his mouth hung open as one entranced. Then he noticed Phil looking at her, and he felt slightly jealous. Phil was his friend, but in this matter he had no friend. The young lady was unaccompanied. He kept his head against the wall and watched her without winking.

Phil noticed Stanley's face and laughed. He said, 'What's wrong with you, boy? Like you under some spell or something?'

Stanley kept serious. In fact, he had hardly heard what Phil said. He was waiting to make a move. The only thing that clicked was an eyelid. As the stranger's eyes glanced at him, he winked so fast that nobody else saw. And nobody else saw when the stranger smiled.

His heart raced giddily. Phil, who was looking at him and did not know what had happened, said, 'But Stan, you's always a cool feller. You don't even know where this pretender come from. Take your time, boy. Take it easy. You watching the pretty face but these strange ladies only have tricks.'

Stanley was only half-hearing his companion because he wasn't even listening. He simply said to himself, 'Pretender? I don't care if she's a pretender or a flash in the pan or whatever you want to call it? All I want is for the music to start up!'

Phil looked at her and looked at Stanley's eyes. He had never seen anybody so love-crazed all of a sudden. Also, most of the men were only pretending to be chatting and having a good time, but were stealing chances to gaze at the strange lady. Not many were paying attention to their own talk. Some were turning around nervously, with strained smiles on their faces, eyeing Stanley, and unashamedly wanting to offer the beautiful young stranger a drink. The musicians were still getting their instruments out of their music boxes, but even these men seemed nervous and when a few of them tried out their trumpets and saxophones they seemed to be reading the notes off the lady's face. Everyone acted as if the night was a special night and this was a special dance, because of the presence of this strange lady. Stanley stood watching them and watching the eyes which had blinked back and the face which had smiled quickly at him. He could hardly wait for the music to start.

For Phil, though, this was no special night. He was furious with

Stanley. He kept telling himself, 'Look at that stupid clown. Making a fool of himself. He doesn't know the silly tramp, but look at him!'

He was so annoyed he left and went out to the verandah to get a little fresh air. And there he contemplated what he called 'the stupidness' that had come over the place. Accidentally, his heart caught the strange lady smiling, and his heart thumped. But she slipped away. And he said to himself, 'It's the night air out here that making me shake so. I so sorry I wasted me precious time to come here with this foolish friend ah mine. Eh, Sah? People with silk and satin and eye-shade and all this blooming nonsense. We should ban strangers from this village dance!'

He leaned against the banister and looked out on the dismal, starless night. There was nothing in front of him but thick high woods. Nobody saw when any car came — if any car came at all, he thought. There, in front of him and lining the forest was the village road, and across the road were a few straggling houses.

Phil thought of his friend again and shook his head. And then he wondered: how come this strange lady came to the dance here to set foolish hearts ablaze? And he said to himself, 'Who is the feller she came with? Where he is? He done know he's the luckiest man in the world so he brought this beauty here to make botheration?'

Then he added, 'What sort ah man is that? I mean, he'll bring something like *this* here, and leave it? He can't appreciate the magic loveliness . . .' Then he stopped short, jolted by his own words. He said hastily, 'Wait, what wrong with you, boy? You is Stan or what? I can't believe those words coming from your mouth!'

As he was thinking this, the music struck up, and to calm his confused mind he got up and went to look. But as he looked it came to him that it was the musicians who were confused, for they began with a *casteeyan*, a giddy Spanish waltz which already had dancers reeling crazily across the floor. In fact, it was *Brisas del Zulia*, they were playing, the craziest of all *casteeyans*, and it looked as if everybody was on the floor. Everybody, but he himself. Indeed, although he was confused and annoyed, even furious, he did mutter, in a part of his mind, 'Phil, you mean you ain't dancing *Brisas*, boy? What wrong with you?'

And it was just around this moment that his head went wild. For he happened to see Stanley, and at that instant he stood gazing in disbelief, his mouth wide open. Not that he had never seen his friend dance before — nor dance with such spirit. It was not that at all. He was flabbergasted to see who Stanley's partner was. Stanley was dancing with the lovely stranger, the glamorous mystery lady that had walked into the dance-hall no one knew from where. Phil's heart thumped hard as his eyes followed the couple. It was as if he was seeing nothing else. The wild music of *Brisas del Zulia* had come to its soft and sweet, almost poetic part, and when he saw Stanley dancing the lady with such romantic tenderness, his heart cried out. And his lips whispered, bitterly, 'Yes, that is yuh life-long sweetheart. Dance she in yuh old clothes!'

For a little while, the music continued calm and sweet, but when it heated up again and got wild, Phil watched the two people swirl about, virtually taking over the hall in what seemed the craziest moment of all. He watched his friend leaping about and he looked at the clothes, but was too bewildered to be amused. Stan's chafed, crinkled-up, patched-up, washed-out blue shirt was out of the pants and seemed to be flying about. The stained khaki pants seemed swept not by a breeze but by a raging wind, as all the other dancers backed off, leaving the floor to Stanley and the lady in velvety green.

There was only music and action and the clatter of high-heeled shoes. All eyes stared at the two dancers. Stanley was now lifting his legs so high and spinning the lady so vigorously that people were continually shifting out of the way — even at the bar. And yet, despite Stanley's flamboyance, his partner looked so elegant and serene it was as if she was just floating in space.

Phil was spellbound. He said to himself, 'What is this? I never knew Stan to be dancing Spanish Waltz. Ay ay! And he dancing this Spanish Waltz so bumptious, as if he own this blooming place. And the music men encouraging him, because they playing this damn waltz so sweet – ah mean, so stupid – I never hear it so before. It good if they even ban them too. Oh, God!'

And as he said 'Oh, God!' there was the feeling of something strange. It was a gentle flow of the music, and as the couple passed near to him, someone cried out, 'But look at these two love-birds!' A big wave of jealousy seemed to knock Phil over. He turned angrily away and glared into the pitch-black night.

After a few minutes a roar of applause made him look round. The set was over and people were swarming around Stanley and the strange lady, congratulating them. Phil said under his breath, 'Life strange, eh? The musicians play out their soul-case, slow and fast music, the good-for-nothing so-and-so putting up his legs and making style. Eh heh? But you think anybody will go and hug up the musicians? Yet this damn worthless, son of a geezer — look at that! People going and fighting to hug them up.' Phil stormed away and went to the darkest corner of the banister.

In the dance-hall Stanley was feeling transported but, with the set over, the place felt so steaming hot he was anxious to get away from the crowd. Sweat was dripping from his forehead and he took out his handkerchief and wiped his forehead and his wet face. The strange, glamorous lady had left her hand in his and his heart was pounding. She was not sweating but he passed his handkerchief over her forehead. Then he looked around the dance-hall, but he did not see his best friend.

'Where's Phil?' he asked himself. He couldn't even remember seeing Phil after the dance started. Phil must have already gone home. He felt bitterly let down. Phil could have hardly been closer to him and this was the chief person he had wanted to be seen by. It was no good relating the story to Phil — he would never believe it. Who could believe? He felt very downcast to think that Phil had not witnessed his moment of glory.

He was thinking this with the crowd still milling around him, and he was beginning to feel mauled and suffocated. When he at last got a break he whispered in the lady's ear, 'Let's go out in the gallery and get some breeze.'

With groans and excuses they eased towards the door, then managed to slip out into the verandah.

Holding his partner tightly in a dark corner of the verandah, he was alone with her and he was tempted to pour his heart out. But he just said, 'You see it cool and nice here? Breeze blowing from the forest, like *Brisas del Zulia*.' What he really wanted to say were three little words, but, although he had rehearsed them over and over again in his mind, he did not have the courage to say them. But his thoughts repeated them all the time, *I love you*. He looked into the bewitching face and felt much too overwhelmed to speak. As a way of making conversation, he said, 'We could stay right here. They looking for us, but let's stay right here in this dark. Until the next set strike up. Oh, God! I wonder if it's intermission. Ah enjoyed that *casteeyan*. You know what we call *casteeyan* here? Holy smoke, it so hot! I ain't even ask you where you come from. You know what we call *casteeyan*? Spanish Waltz. Oh, I love that so much . . . and I . . .' He did not have the courage to add, 'love you.'

The strange lady laughed eerily and her cackle seemed to dissolve on the wind and into the night. The whole verandah was dark, but Stanley, huddled up in the darkest corner, could see the glistening of her teeth. Stanley murmured, 'I so like to dance the *casteeyan* with you. You feel so light it's as if I ain't holding nothing. We have to dance the next *casteeyan* again, please.'

She laughed, and this time her laughter was like the tinkling of silver bells in the distance, and in a strange sort of way it gave Stanley the feeling of more enchantment and more helplessness. The lady broke off laughing and said, 'What is the time? It must be nearly midnight and I have to go.' And she burst out in soft laughter again and her high-pitched voice said, '. . . next *casteeyan*? . . . next *casteeyan* . . . ?' There were more waves of laughter and the sound seemed to cling to the air, then fade and die.

Close by in the dark, Phil began growing concerned. And now, with this last peal of laughter he straightened up. He was thinking hard. There was something strangely familiar. This lady had just said she had to leave at midnight. Midnight? This woman came as if from nowhere, had the whole place under a spell, she had Stanley going crazy, the musicians going wild, and now she said she had to leave at midnight! To him, the case became as clear as crystal.

He eased nearer the couple, screened by the pitch-blackness. He was sweating now — sweating with a little fear. Although he had told himself that the case was as clear as crystal, he kept saying to himself, 'I wonder if she is . . . wonder if . . . wonder if she really is . . .'

If she was what he was thinking she was, then his friend could easily be doomed. Lost forever. He pondered on the lady's words and they seemed to correspond with everything he had heard about these creatures. He did not only think of her words but he thought of her laughter, and more than ever, of her dress: hat with silken brim, light green zecac gown, long, and covering the feet. Yes, covering the feet because the right foot was . . . He could not imagine this creature had a cow's hoof.

Nearby sobbing interrupted Phil's thoughts. Not the sobs of the lady but of Stanley. Phil was on the point of blurting out, 'What happen, Stan?' but he stopped himself.

He did not know what to do. He could not see his friend in such distress and remain quiet. Yet if he had spoken they could have easily thought he had been eavesdropping. He stood up stiffly against the wall, while Stanley's words came. He could not help hearing. 'Please let me go with you. Please, my angel. I love you so bad — I don't know why. I don't know what happen. Please let me go with you because I just can't live without you . . .'

Soft, unearthly laughter filtered into the air, and the lady's voice said, 'Okay, you want to go with me? Let's see. When the clock strikes 12 we have to go. What is the time?'

Phil was on the point of crying out, 'Don't go with her!' when he heard the sound of matches. It was Stanley who had taken out his match-box, but the lady frantically threw herself against him, 'No! Don't strike that match!'

Stanley said, 'But you want to know the time!'

She was holding the hand which held the box of matches. 'Don't strike that match. Please! Don't do that!'

And now Phil was sure he was right. She was exactly what he

thought she was. He quickly pulled out a box of his own matches and as he struck one he screamed, 'This is the time!'

When the flame lit up the dark verandah there was so much commotion that not even the noise of the wildest *casteeyan* could have drowned it out. People rushed into the verandah, and when they switched on the light they saw a trail of smoke with the sweeping velvety gown disappearing into the forest across the road.

Phil shouted at Stan in front of all the crowd, 'You like to show-off on me. You don't know me when you see a nice face. You dancing up and spinning with yuh legs high in the air. And the so-called angel cosy in yuh arms. Tha's how you like it. And you passing by me and you too proud to watch and yuh don't know me name; you don't know who the hell is Phil. But it's Phil who save you tonight. You wouldn't listen, you wouldn't hear nobody but the angel, not so? But it's Phil who have to hide in the gallery and save you, boy. And it isn't saving you from the angel, you know, but saving you from the devil. Yes, it's Phil who had to come to yuh aid tonight to save you from la diablesse!'

The crowd, speechless, just stood staring at the forest.

8

The spell of the Shango

The Shango dancers were whirling around in a frenzy. The drummers — three of them — were pounding out the rhythms on the drums, and the loud, blending voices seemed to shake the leaves of the coconut trees. Margaret and I were spending our honeymoon in the village, and when she heard the drums, she came excitedly calling me. I was not very enthusiastic, but nevertheless I walked with her up the lonely road from the beach to the Shango tent.

We saw the dancers, women clad in white, whirling around and singing; and the drummers, big brawny men, sweating, their muscles shimmering and throbbing with the drums.

I looked at them, unmoved, but Margaret said, 'You know how long I've been hearing about these people? Oh, God! This is what I've always wanted to see. This is the real Africa.'

'Which Africa?' I did not want to hurt her but she knew what I meant.

She said, 'Okay, I know. I know it's sentimental, but to me this is the real Africa. The dancers and the drums. This is what I think of when I think of Africa.'

I did not say anything for a while. I never could understand how Margaret, who had spent so many years in England, could yearn for something which to me was the very opposite of progress. The Africa that I wanted to see was an Africa of industry and sophistication, but Margaret was mad about folklore and seemed satisfied with things like the Shango. We had quarrelled about this sort of thing before, so I was careful about what I said now. I wanted to stave off our first tiff of married life.

The dancers whirled round, chanting plaintively, and the whole atmosphere seemed to be charged with emotion. There was the Shango queen herself, wearing a red head-tie and wheeling round and round on one spot and with her face entranced. The sound of the chanting seemed touching, and in a sense, blood-curdling, but what were stranger to me were the drums. Oddly enough, they seemed to touch the very soul. They were so expressive it was as if they wanted to say something.

Margaret whispered, 'This is the sort of thing I always wanted to see. Funny, eh? We saw so much of Africa in London — on the stage, in films, and in all sorts of things. But nothing of the genuine Africa, like this. This is the real thing. I could feel it inside me. This is *me*.'

'Well join the Shango, girl,' I said, smiling, watching to see how she would take it. 'If you are a child of Africa, as you always say, then join the Shango. Don't get me wrong. I'm a child of Africa too, but not of *this* Africa, Meg.' She looked at me. I felt we might quarrel. Nevertheless I went on, 'I can't feel anything for *this* Africa. I want to see progress. I want to see African engineers, African surgeons. I want to see Africans swelling the universities. In other words, I want to see Africa get bright and modern. This primitive thing with drums and rituals is not the Africa for me.'

Her head had turned to the drummers and the dancers. There was no danger of a honeymoon quarrel, for she was so enrapt with what was happening before her that she had little time for me. The ritual had got to fever pitch and the Shango queen was now convulsing in frenzy and spinning with a basin of water on her head.

Margaret said excitedly, 'Look, this is the time for the sacrifice. They're bringing out the goat.'

I turned my head away in disgust. I knew Margaret well, and I knew that, with all the talk, she could not face that cruel sacrifice of the goat. Because she did not like to see blood.

But after a moment she turned and held me on my shoulder. She said, 'What happen, Ritchie? You squeamish? This is all part of the ritual.'

I was shocked. She half-turned and looked at me and said, 'Ritchie, isn't this amazing? Think of the slaves who brought this with them from Africa so long ago. And they passed this thing on and on and yet it remained intact. This, what yuh seeing here, is the genuine thing. The real Africa. I could feel it. Land of my fathers. Tears coming to me eyes, boy. It's amazing how nobody forgot anything.'

I said, 'And it's amazing how nobody learned anything either. This is the same old thing of hundreds of years ago. Tears coming to me eyes too. Because when will we develop? Come on, man, Margaret, we have to come out into the modern world.'

She seemed to be barely paying attention to me, but she retorted, 'Modern world? What's wrong with you? Don't make me laugh. Listen to those drums. Yuh listening? Those drums talking, boy. This thing is timeless. There's no past, no present. This is vibrant, Ritchie. You should be proud. This is us.'

There was no argument to convince Margaret. By now the whole tent was in a frenzy and I was absorbed in looking at the steps of the dancers. At the way the women were drifting and yet did not collide. At how the men in their white-drill shorts, their red merinos, and their deep voices were floating around like dream-gods. To my ear the drums were becoming more and more like voices, and the singing more and more plaintive, and as if touching on the soul.

I said, 'What I find, Meg . . .'

'Stop talking.'

'But it's something I want to tell you. The people . . .'

I stopped. She was not listening. She was enrapt in the ritual unfolding before her eyes. The singing seemed to rise as if with power and glory and, although I tried to turn my mind off it, it seemed to be compelling me to listen. The drums themselves seemed to be throbbing inside my very abdomen and I felt so confused and strange I wanted to go home. I turned my head away towards the coconut trees and the sea, but slowly my mind wandered back to the white-clad women who were now bending so gracefully in a semi-circle. I looked at them with their eyes half-shut, and swaying and dancing round in circles. I saw the Shango queen swirling in the centre of the ring as if she was in a trance, tottering as though she was going to fall and, as I gazed at her, my eyes caught two men in blood-spattered shirts and three-quarter length trousers, moving as if lost in a spirit world. More to pass the time and to stave off the confused feeling, I burst out laughing.

Margaret turned swiftly to me. 'What you doing? Ritchie, you mad? Please don't upset the spirits. For Godsake don't laugh at the rites of Africa.'

'But it's not rites. Look at those two funny fellers over there.'

'They aren't funny. This is their way. This is the way of the Shango.'

'They aren't funny? Look at them good.' And I could not help laughing again.

The drummers were sitting facing me on the other side of the tent, and now I saw one of them, a big muscular one in the centre

— I saw him stop drumming and now he was scowling at me. I wanted to go over to him and say, 'Sorry, pal.' But Margaret held me back.

He remained looking fixedly at me, the scowl not leaving his face, and then all of a sudden he began to beat again, but this time as if in a rage, quickening the tempo, making his singers scream, even screech, as if wailing in pain.

I said, 'Margaret, Oh God. Let's go. These damn drums as if they beating inside me. These women ain't singing, they crying. This ain't no place for me. I can't take it. Let's go.'

I heard Margaret's voice as though it were coming from a distance. She was saying, 'This is Shango . . . and you have to take it . . . or leave it . . . This is Shango singing . . . right down from the soul . . .'

And then she cried, 'Good God! Something happening to you, boy? Ritchie, what happening?'

I could not answer. I tried, but I could not. Her voice sounded as if it was coming from the wind and the sea. And then it seemed to trail off. And all I knew was a terrible shaking of the body, and then it was as if a whole ocean had broken over me.

When I came to myself again, I was lying inside the Shango tent, and they were dashing water on my face and holding a glass of water to my mouth, trying to force me to drink it. When I opened my eyes, I heard someone say, 'It's okay, now. He revive.' I looked around and it was the big stout Shango queen herself. She had her arm around Margaret and they and a number of others were bending over me.

When Margaret saw my eyes open, she gasped with relief. She cried, 'Thank goodness. Heavens. Oh, Saviour. Thank you, Lord.' Then she threw herself on me. 'Oh, Ritchie! I thought you'd never revive.'

The Shango queen said, 'Look! See and get him home. When you get home, wash his face with a little dew and rain-water. You might have to wait till fore-day morning.'

They pulled me up to a sitting position, and they tried to get

me to stand and I stumbled, and then I got up on my own two legs. I was feeling weak and shaky.

After we said goodbye to the Shango people, we took the lonely moonlit road along the beach.

When we had walked a little way I said, 'Margaret, what happened to me? Ah fainted or what?'

She did not talk. I was feeling too dazed to ask her anything else.

As the sea-breeze hit me, my head seemed to be clearing up. Margaret stopped holding me now but she was walking close by, watching me in case I stumbled or collapsed. I was feeling fagged out.

We walked in silence for a while and then she said, 'Boy, you gave me a surprise. Although you passed out at the end, you made me feel so proud tonight.' She looked at me and beamed.

I watched her. I knew something had happened, but I was afraid to ask her what. At length I said, 'Meg, please. What happened?'

She hesitated a little and then she said, 'Ritchie, all through these years you were either making a joke with me or making the monkey out of me. I never knew the truth about you. But I ain't vexed, because tonight you made me feel so proud. You tried to pretend you didn't like Shango, and you really had me believing you. But boy, the way you danced tonight, and threw up your hands in the air and called upon Ogun and Iemanja, you brought tears to everybody's eyes. Even to the Shango queen who was in the ring with you.'

She continued, 'The only thing I didn't like was that Shango drummer riding you. The big burly one. And you let him do it, and you were even dancing with him.'

I shook my head. It was no use talking. I did not know anything of what she was talking about.

She shook that off her mind and continued, 'But even if you were hiding things from me, I feel satisfied. You asking me what happened? what happened? Just because you know you had the whole Shango yard spellbound. It's only coming towards the last when Ogun came for you, and you had to leave with Iemanja.

Ritchie, I feel so good, you wouldn't believe. But you passed out, fainting for such a long time that I thought you wasn't going to wake up?' she laughed nervously.

But I said nothing. It was the first time in my life I had gone to a Shango tent. I just looked at her blankly.

She said, 'I could now see why you used to talk like that. Yes, I could see now. Because you have a weakness for the Shango and you trying to keep away. But why? Not because you belong to me that I'm saying this, but you is the best Shango dancer I ever saw. True. Look, do this for me, Ritchie. Don't keep away, please, because you too good. Boy, I so glad I married you.'

I walked on, staring blindly into space. My brain felt exhausted and my body was as harassed as though I had been a beast of burden. I walked weakly on to our honeymoon house near the beach.

9

The silk cotton trees of Sangre Grande

From the time Pa Harris moved into the area, he did not like the idea of the silk cotton trees standing there. He did not like the look of those two huge trees, with the girth of the trunks more formidable than he had ever seen. And they were so tall that their branches seemed to scrape the sky. But what was more, those trees lay on either side of the road he had to pass every day — the road to Sangre Chiquito, where he had bought the piece of land.

From the time he had moved here and seen those trees, he had grown depressed. He had kept murmuring to himself, 'Soucouyant trees, ligahoo trees. Ah don't know why they harbouring these trees here — that's encouraging evil!'

At last he decided that the only solution was to have a talk with the Ward Officer. One day he walked round by the Police Station and went to the Warden's Office.

He spoke and the young Ward Officer was amused but seemed to be listening intently. At last, when Pa Harris was finished, the Ward Officer looked up and said, 'When?'

'Up to last night,' said Pa Harris. 'Up to last night when I passed here. I saw the thing plain, plain. I tell you it was not a mistake — it was a real spirit. The thing was all in white.' He was trying to tremble.

The Ward Officer laughed. The old man was talking as though he really believed what he was saying. He looked at the old man's face and he said to himself, 'Nothing will change these country people. Just imagine, a man in his right mind talking about real spirit. As if spirits could be real.'

He got up and put his hand on the old man's shoulder. He said, 'Mr Harris, I don't know what to tell you! I don't know. If I talk about people believing in all kinda superstition, it wouldn't make any difference to you. It wouldn't change yuh beliefs. Look, I already realise that straight talk wouldn't make any difference. You done steeped in yuh beliefs. So I can't make no impression. You can't stop people believing in these things because these silly ideas, sorry, I mean these things with us for so long. Even me own wife believe in douen and ligahoo and la diablesse . . .'

'So la diablesse ain't real? Pa Harris interrupted heatedly. 'Ligahoo ain't real! La diablesse ain't — look up to night before . . .'

The Ward Officer laughed softly and he sat down again. He said, 'Take it easy,' without looking at the old man. He was looking at the floor. But after a few seconds he looked up, and he said with a surprisingly firm voice, 'Look, old man, I'll tell you a thing or two. You could take it or leave it, but I'll tell you. I ain't going to beat about no bush, I'll tell you like it is. It ain't have no soucouyant, no ligahoo, no spirit, no douen, no Papa Bois. It ain't have nothing like that.'

Pa Harris looked at him with a shocked face. He was speechless. Then he said, 'But Ward Officer, but I saw it. I saw the spirit with these two eyes. Look, Mr Gentleman, I know you is a young feller and you don't believe what old people say, but don't tell me I didn't see it!'

'I ain't saying you didn't see something. Of course you saw something. But it must be some fig-leaf or so and you say is spirit.'

'That wasn't no fig-leaf. The thing was like a man, and dressed all in white. I was coming home from a friend house in Sangre Chiquito. I was working on me piece of land whole morning, and I went by this friend and then I was going home. It was only nine o'clock. From the time I hit the Sangre Chiquito bridge, I see that white thing. When ah walked a little nearer, I saw it didn't have no head. So I stand up, me foot feeling heavy. From the time I stand up, the thing make a step towards me. I had to run and bawl.'

The young Ward Officer laughed so loudly that the whole office looked around. He put his hands to his mouth quickly. After a while, the Ward Officer turned to the old man but he could not speak, he was laughing so much. At last he said, 'Mr . . . What's you name again?'

'Harris.'

'Mr Harris, you come here to kill me with laugh or what! Is some fig-leaf or something what make you run. Because those things could look white in the night. Some fig-leaf the wind blow. Look here, you is an old man already and I can't change you. But to cut down those trees, Mr Harris! You watching those two lovely silk-cotton trees there and saying they encouraging soucouyant and ligahoo, and spirit! I don't know what to tell you again. Okay, suppose I ask you what is a ligahoo, you could tell me?'

'Ligahoo? Ligahoo is a man who does turn to animal. Ligahoo is a thing that does pull chain in the night. Mr Gentleman, you never see a ligahoo yet?'

The young Ward Officer could not help bursting out into laughter again. Then he said, 'Mr Harris, I just won't say no more. Because your kinda world is not mine. You believe in all sorta superstition like ligahoo and spirit. You talk about Sangre Chiquito — there's where I live. And I pass those silk cotton trees day and night. All hours. You think I have time to see ligahoo and spirit? You think I have time to believe in that kinda thing? The only spirit I scared of is the one with the head. One like you and me.'

He laughed, but the old man did not laugh. All the old man did was nod, with his hat in his hand, and get up. And he said, 'Thank you, Mr Ward Officer.' And he went out through the door.

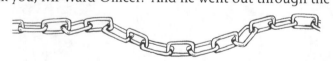

Out in the street in the sunshine, Pa Harris stood up and looked at the silk cotton trees. As he looked at the massive trunks towering above the houses and the big trees, he felt as if there was a fluttering in his belly. He did not have to ask himself, as always, why did they have to have those two trees right there beside the road. Because he was already resolved to get rid of them. For it was people like the Ward Officer who were harbouring those trees, bringing all sorts of douens, and ligahoo, and la diablesse right into the Sangre Grande.

He stood there for a moment looking at the silk cotton trees and working out his plan. At the same time he was thinking of Sangre Chiquito. It was broad daylight — only about ten or half-past ten in the morning. But he did not relish the idea of passing between those trees to go up to Sangre Chiquito.

But if he had to go, he had to go. But first he would have to go up home to collect the things he would need. His head was hot with plans as he crossed the street by the roundabout and headed up Ojoe Road.

As he walked up the road, he smiled wryly. He was not a man to resort to tricks but those trees just had to go. Otherwise he could never remain in Sangre Grande. The young Ward Officer had to be taught a lesson. He had to be made to learn and learn fast.

Pa Harris reached home, collected his garden implements, and immediately left for Sangre Chiquito. As he turned to go up the winding road, he started to recite the prayer 'Magnificat,' to ward off the evil from the silk cotton trees.

It was only a week after this when the young Ward Officer emerged from the Ascot Cinema and was heading home for Sangre Chiquito. The night was black and the show finished so late that, apart from the crowd that left the cinema, all Sangre Grande seemed asleep.

When he reached the roundabout by the Police Station, he

noticed he was the only one going along the road to Sangre Chiquito, so he relaxed, and even began jay-walking along the pavement.

Just then, he heard the jangle of a chain behind him. He looked back but did not see anything. But after a moment he heard the chain again, this time loud, passing on the other side of the road.

His heart began to thump. At first he had thought the jangling of the chain might have come from some cow or donkey which had broken loose — but it could not be, for he had not heard any hooves. His heart was still pounding. His brain seemed to go wild. 'I wonder what's this?' he thought, 'I wonder what this is!'

Now he heard the chain in the distance where the silk cotton trees were, and he said to himself, 'That's funny. Some of these old people does talk sense, you know. They say it have good and it have evil. I wonder if this is . . . I wonder if it's anything superstitious.'

As he approached the silk cotton trees, he slowed down his steps. An owl screeching in the branches made him jump. He stopped. Then he began walking again, timidly.

When he reached that part of the road flanked by the trees, his heart began racing more than ever. Now he heard the chain rush past on the other side and his head went wild, and his heart raced with fear.

He tried to pass the silk cotton trees quickly, but as he nearly got past he heard a voice say clearly, 'Ward

Officer.' As he turned round in the darkness, he could see nothing but flowing white robes.

'Oh, God!' he screamed and bolted wildly down the road.

Pa Harris found those robes too cumbersome. He chased him just a little way, then stood up.

The next morning, Monday, the Ward Officer was at his desk early. He was whistling cheerily, despite aching legs and a bruised elbow. And he was scribbling in one of his note-books. Then he called for one of his labourers.

When the man came, the Ward Officer said, 'Look, Braff, do this for me right away.'

The labourer went up to him.

The Ward Officer said, 'Take this slip to Caines and tell him to arrange immediately for the felling of those two silk cotton trees.'

The labourer was startled. He said, 'The silk cotton trees, Sir? The ones on the main road? They there for years. They ain't do nobody nothing.'

The Ward Officer laughed. 'You got it, Braff. That's exactly what it is. They there for years. And they ain't do nobody anything — not yet. But nobody knows when they'll come crashing down on some bus, or on some crowd. And you know what will happen then? Then they'll do a lot of people something. And then everybody would be after the Ward Officer's head. See what I mean? So fix that up for me, Braff, good man. Let's take in front before in front take us.'

About the Author

Michael Anthony writes novels, short stories, and historical works. To date he has produced 24 books. These comprise ten novels and two books of short stories, ten historical works, and a book of brief biographies.

Born in 1930, he began by writing poems in his late teens and early 20s, and many of these poems appeared in Trinidad newspapers.

He also became very interested in writing short stories and when he went to England in 1954 he contributed both short stories and poems to a BBC 'Calling the West Indies' programme called *Caribbean Voices*.

He published his first novel, *The Games were Coming*, in 1963.

His main works have been the novels: *The Year in San Fernando, Green Days by the River, All that Glitters* and *The High Tide of Intrigue;* a study of the Carnivals of the 20th century, called *Parade of the Carnivals of Trinidad and Tobago;* and *The Historical Dictionary of Trinidad and Tobago,* which highlights all aspects of the country's history.

The Year in San Fernando and *Green Days by the River* have been regularly set as literature by the Caribbean Examinations Council.

He has lived in London, Rio de Janeiro (Brazil), and is now at home in Trinidad.

Michael Anthony, who is holder of the Humming Bird Gold Medal, a Trinidad national award, was given the honorary degree of D.Litt (Doctor of Letters) by the University of the West Indies in 2003.

His pride and joy is his family: his wife, Yvette; two daughters: Jennifer, a teacher, and Sandra, a medical student; two sons, both doing law; and four grandchildren: Julien Michael, Marie Ann, Amber and Michael.